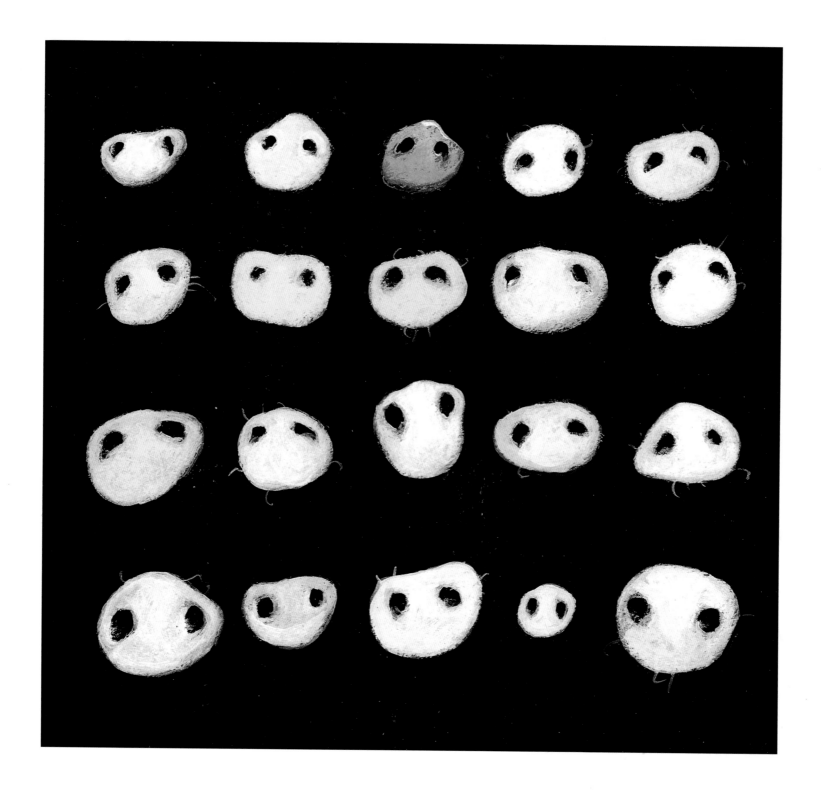

John A. Rowe **Peter Piglet**

Copyright © 1996 by Michael Neugebauer Verlag AG,
Gossau Zürich, Switzerland. First published in Switzerland
under the title *Ferkel Ferdinand*. English translation
copyright © 1996 by North-South Books Inc. All rights
reserved. No part of this book may be reproduced or
utilized in any form or by any means, electronic or
mechanical, including photocopying, recording, or any
information storage and retrieval system, without
permission in writing from the publisher.

First published in the United States, Canada, Great Britain, Australia,
and New Zealand in 1996 by North-South Books, an imprint of Nord-Süd
Verlag AG, Gossau Zürich, Switzerland. Distributed in the United States
by North-South Books Inc., New York.

Library of Congress Cataloging-in-Publication Data is available.
A CIP catalogue record for this book is available from The British Library.
ISBN 1-55858-660-1 (trade binding) 10 9 8 7 6 5 4 3 2 1
ISBN 1-55858-661-X (library binding) 10 9 8 7 6 5 4 3 2 1
Printed in Italy

For more information about our books, and the authors and artists
who create them, visit our web site: http://www.northsouth.com

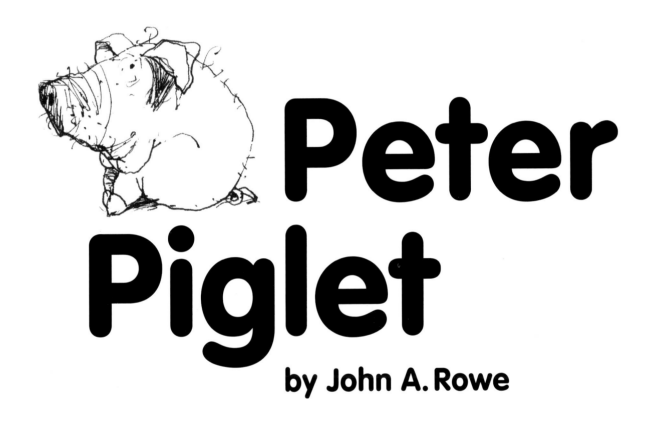

Peter Piglet

by John A. Rowe

A Michael Neugebauer Book
North-South Books · New York · London

Peter Piglet is a chubby fellow with no nose to speak of and a tail like a corkscrew. He is as soft as raspberries and as pink as a rose. He lives in the woods at the edge of my garden.

One morning while Peter snoozed beneath a warm summer sky, along came a gentle breeze filled with secret perfumes and the buzz of busy bees. The breeze tickled the hairs on his nose and woke him.

He rolled over among the yellow dandelions and stretched. It was a lovely day for a walk. So Peter Piglet trotted off through the woods that sunny morning, and he cast a big shadow beneath the mighty oaks.

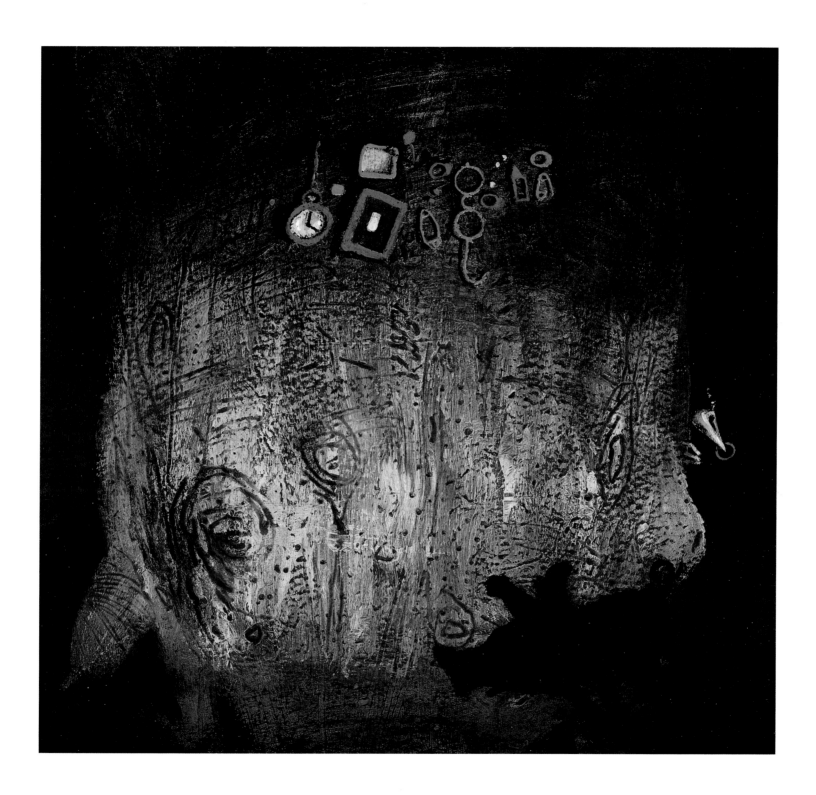

Before long he came upon a pile of sticks decorated with acorns and blackbird feathers. Being naturally curious, he stuck his nose right in and sniffed.

He could hardly believe what he found! There, lying neatly side by side, was a pair of beautiful golden shoes!

Peter sat back and scratched his head. He hardly dared to breathe in case it was all a dream. But dragonfly wings hummed in his ear—he was wide awake!

"Oh, how beautiful!" he whispered. Then, before Peter knew what had happened, he had slipped one foot in . . . then the other.

Clouds in the shapes of wonderful shoes drifted across the blue sky, and the skylarks sang dancing tunes. Peter Piglet was so happy.

Peter had never worn shoes before, and at first he found it very difficult to walk in them. But he kept trying until he became quite an expert.

And as he did, he grew to love those golden shoes more and more.

He went off to show the shoes to that pincushion on legs, Hedgehog.

"Oh, yes," agreed Hedgehog, "they do make you look rather nice indeed!"

"And look how well I can walk, too!" cried Peter proudly. And he proceeded to show Hedgehog a few fancy steps.

"Oh, yes," agreed Hedgehog, "you do walk rather well indeed!"

And so Peter Piglet spent the rest of the afternoon showing Hedgehog the finer points of walking, and dancing, and skipping, and hopping, and climbing, and even *swimming* in his golden shoes.

And in no time at all the Man in the Moon was looking down, and he bathed Peter with his shiny light.

Poor Peter was exhausted—and so were his feet! Placing the golden shoes by his head for safekeeping, he curled up among the foxgloves and ferns and fell into a deep sleep.

That night Peter Piglet dreamed of princes and swirling ballrooms, and his little pink legs danced and jiggled about—keeping time with some unknown, dreamy music. His snoring could be heard for miles. The early-morning dew fell silently and settled on Peter like powdered sugar on a marshmallow. Sleepy green caterpillars swayed ever so gently on silken threads as early birds dug for worms.

Peter Piglet awoke early, and a moment later he turned as white as a snowflake. His golden shoes were gone– vanished! What a shock!

Peter searched high and low. He climbed trees, stuck his head down rabbit holes, but he couldn't find those shoes anywhere. Peter asked Owl, that fine-feathered old hooter, if he had seen the shoes with his big eyes.

He asked Mole, that gentleman in the velvet waistcoat, if he had heard anything about the shoes with his sharp ears. He even asked Hedgehog, that old hairbrush with a nose, if he had smelled them. But nobody could help him.

Poor Peter Piglet was so sad. He looked down at his bare feet, and a big tear rolled down his wrinkly nose and fell to the ground with a loud plop.

He sat down on top of a hill and sighed deeply. Clouds in the shape of tears rolled across the gloomy sky while blackbirds called sadly to each other. Peter didn't know if he could live without those golden shoes.

His life had become ordinary.

Suddenly a tiny voice said, "Just look at my magnificent house!"

Peter jumped up in surprise and looked around, but he saw no one.

"No, down here!" called the tiny voice.

Peter looked down. "Why . . . that's one of my golden . . ."

"Isn't it wonderful!" said an old, wrinkly tortoise. "I had lost my house in a storm and I had nowhere to live. Then I found this beautiful golden palace—now I'm so happy!"

"B-b-but . . ." stuttered Peter Piglet.

"I know," said Tortoise with a smile. "It's only an old shoe, but it has saved my life, and now I couldn't be happier."

"Er . . . but . . ." said Peter. He just didn't know what to say.

"Well, good-bye, Peter Piglet," said Tortoise, and he disappeared into the ferns again.

"Well, I never!" said Peter. "A tortoise in a golden palace!"

Before Peter had even caught his breath, he heard another soft voice—"Look! Just look at my fabulous cradle!"
Peter spun around. He peered down into the ferns, but he couldn't see a soul. Then he looked up and—"Why . . . that's my other golden . . ."
"Isn't it wonderful?" said a shiny blackbird. "I lost my nest in a strong wind, and my children had nowhere to live. Then I found this beautiful golden cradle—now we're all so happy!"
"But . . . but . . ." sputtered Peter Piglet.
"I know," said Blackbird with a smile. "It's only an old shoe, but it has saved our lives and we couldn't be happier."
"Er . . . yes, but . . ." gasped Peter. "I . . . er . . . yes, that's wonderful, but . . ."
And suddenly Peter Piglet saw that it really *was* wonderful! Tortoise and Blackbird were both so happy, and Peter was happy for them.

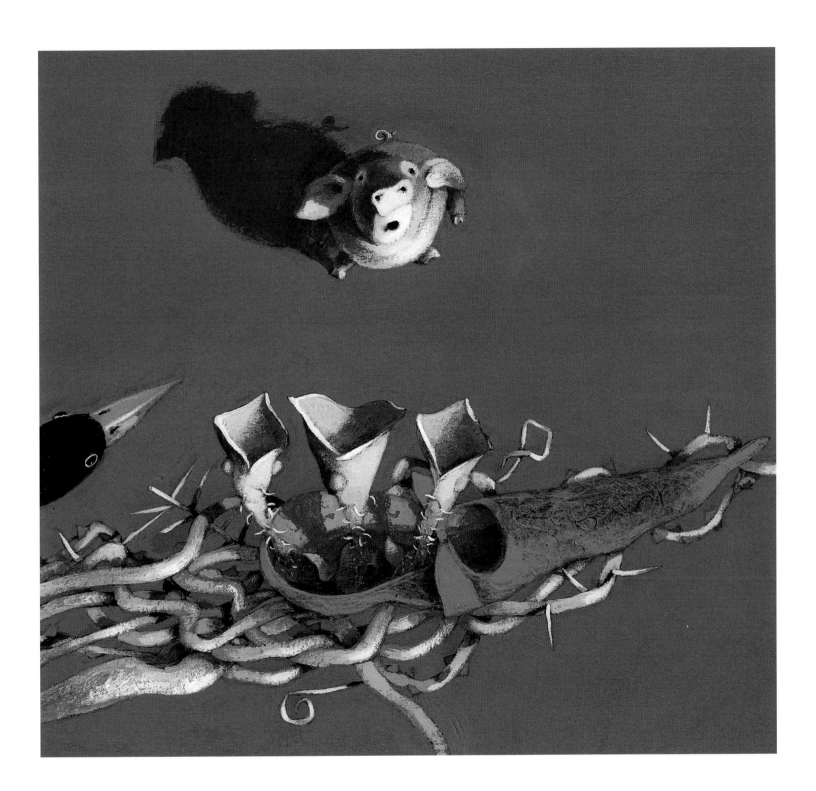

As Peter Piglet trotted off that sunny new day, he decided that life wasn't ordinary after all, and that for a little pig, it's much easier to walk without golden shoes!

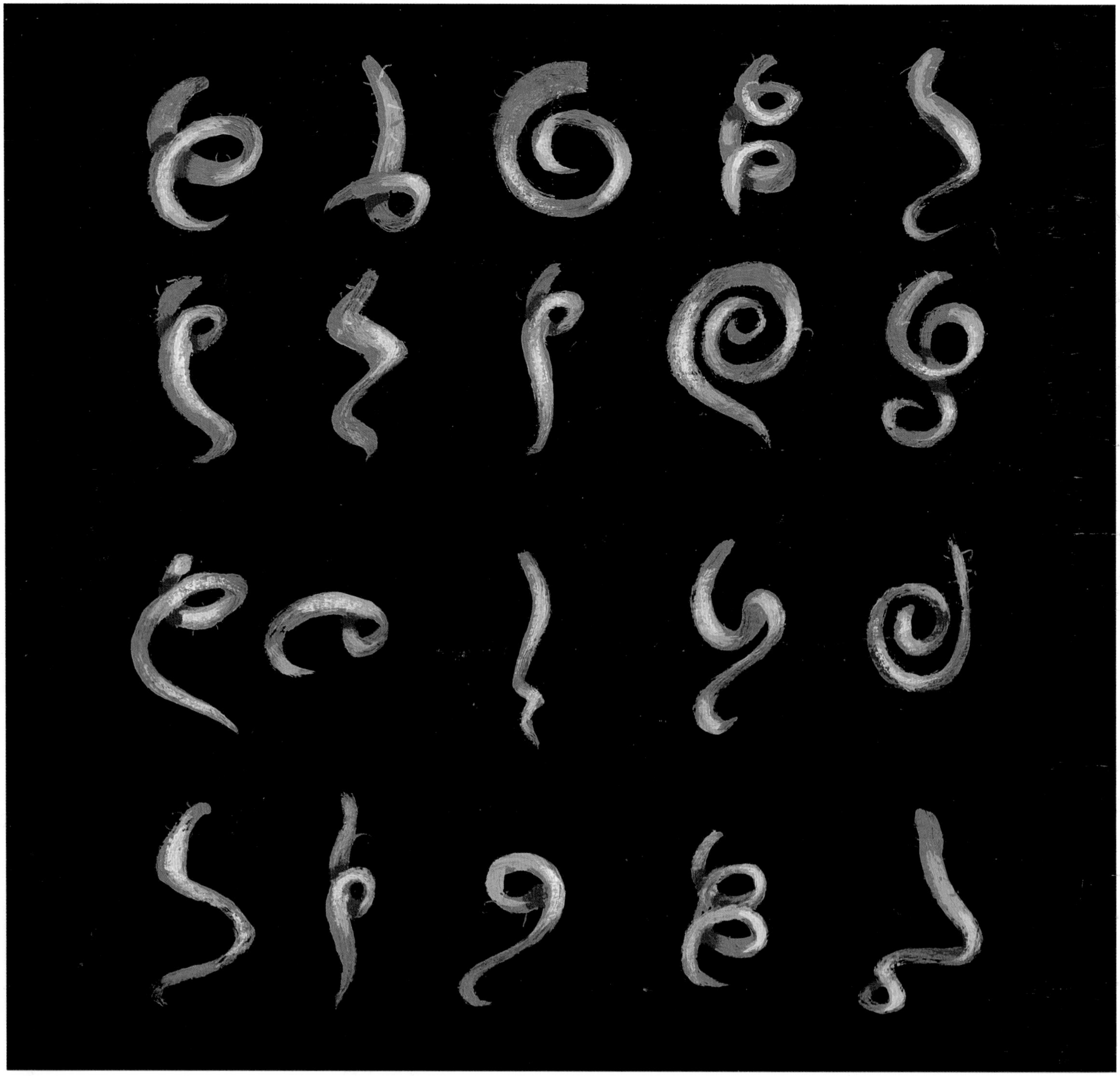